2/02

Green Light Readers

For the new reader who's ready to GO!

Amazing adventures await every young child who is eager to read.
Green Light Readers encourage children to explore, to imagine, and to grow through books. Created for beginning readers at two levels of skill, these lively illustrated stories have been carefully developed to reinforce reading basics taught at school and to make reading a fun and rewarding experience for children and grown-ups to share outside the classroom.

The grades and ages within each skill level are general guidelines only, and books included in both levels may feature any or all of the bulleted characteristics. When choosing a book for a new reader, remember that every child progresses at his or her own pace—be patient and supportive as the magic of reading takes hold.

1 Buckle up!
Kindergarten–Grade 1: Developing reading skills, ages 5–7
- Short, simple stories • Fully illustrated • Familiar objects and situations
- Playful rhythms • Spoken language patterns of children
- Rhymes and repeated phrases • Strong link between text and art

2 Start the engine!
Grades 1–2: Reading with help, ages 6–8
- Longer stories, including nonfiction • Short chapters
- Generously illustrated • Less-familiar situations
- More fully developed characters • Creative language, including dialogue
- More subtle link between text and art

Green Light Readers incorporate characteristics detailed in the Reading Recovery model used by educators to assess the readability of texts through the end of first grade. Guidelines for reading levels for these readers have been developed with assistance from Mary Lou Meerson. An educational consultant, Ms. Meerson has been a classroom teacher, a language arts coordinator, an elementary school principal, and a university professor.

Published in collaboration with Harcourt School Publishers

Ariane Dewey and Jose Aruego

SPLASH!

Green Light Readers
Harcourt, Inc.
San Diego   New York   London

www.harcourt.com

First Green Light Readers edition 2001
Green Light Readers is a trademark of Harcourt, Inc.,
registered in the United States of America and/or other jurisdictions.

Library of Congress Cataloging-in-Publication Data
Dewey, Ariane.
Splash!/by Ariane Dewey and Jose Aruego.
p. cm.
"Green Light Readers."
Summary: Two clumsy bears join in fishing fun at the river.
[1. Bears—Fiction. 2. Clumsiness—Fiction. 3. Fishing—Fiction.]
I. Aruego, Jose. II. Title. III. Green Light Reader.
PZ7.D5228Sp 2001
[E]—dc21   00-9723
ISBN 0-15-216256-9
ISBN 0-15-216262-3 (pb)

A C E G H F D B
A C E G H F D B (pb)

"Wake up, you big fur ball!" Nelly yelled. She gave Sam a shake.

"Don't be a pest, Nelly," Sam growled.
"I'm dreaming about fat, floppy fish."
"Let's go find some!" Nelly said.

Nelly rushed out of their cave.
Sam jumped up and ran after her.

"Is that sound a splash?" asked Sam. "I bet it's bears," said Nelly. "Let's hurry, before all the fish are gone."

Together, they ran to the river.

The river was full of bears catching fish.
"Oh no," the bears groaned. "Here come
Sam and Nelly."

"What kind of mess will they make this time?" said one bear.

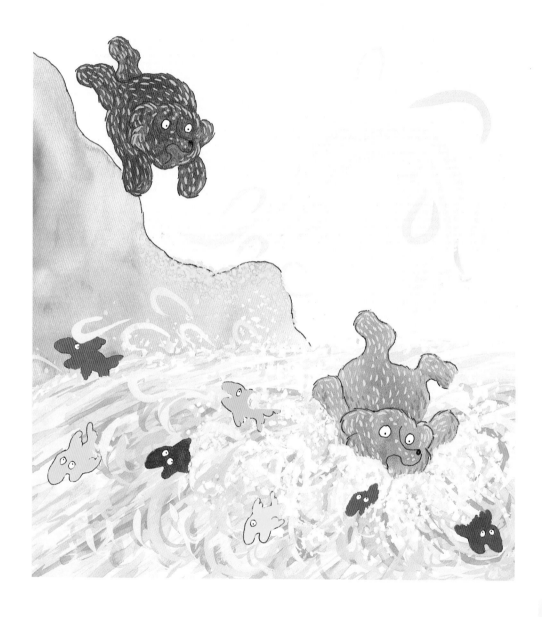

Nelly slipped on a wet rock. She fell into the river. *Splash!*

"I'll save you!" Sam yelled, slipping after her.

Splash again!
Together, Nelly and Sam made a wave
that tipped over ten bears.

"Why are you two always so clumsy?"
growled one bear.
"We'll be more careful!" said Sam.

"OK, OK. You can fish with us," said the other bears. "But for once, try to behave."

Sam and Nelly sat very still with the other bears. While they were sitting, lots of fish swam by.

The bears had never seen so many fish
in one place. All they could hear was
the sound of swishing fins.

"Quick! Get them before they're gone!" Sam yelled. Hungry bears snapped at the fish. The river was a jumble of fins and fur. The bears had fun chasing the fish.

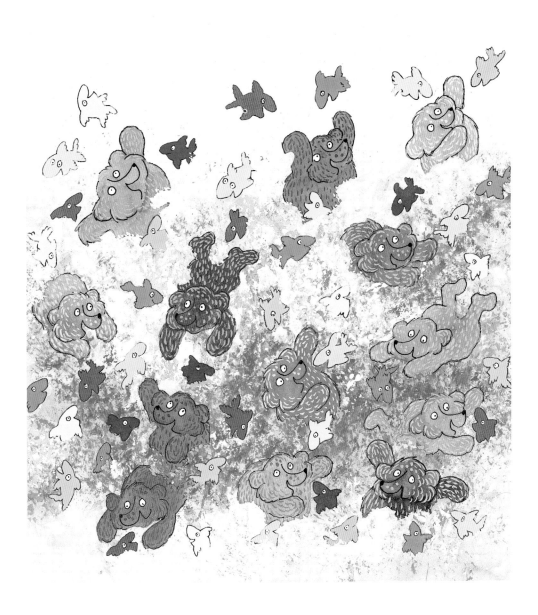

And the fish had fun racing away.
They swam to the bottom of a safe
deep lake.

All of the bears had so much fun, they forgot they were hungry. Sam and Nelly walked home to their cave.

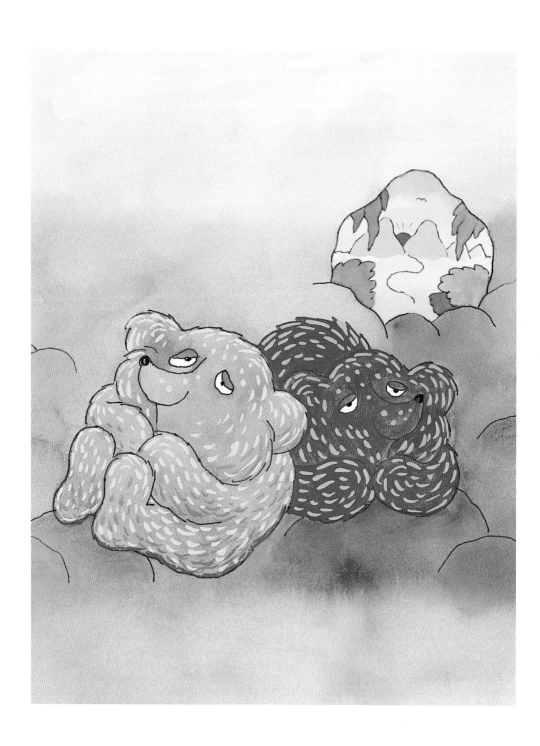

"We are clumsy," said Sam.
"But we do have fun!" said Nelly.
Now all they needed was a good
long nap!

Meet the Author-Illustrators

© 1999 Todd Bigelow/Black Star

© 1999 Todd Bigelow/Black Star

Ariane Dewey

Jose Aruego

Ariane Dewey and Jose Aruego like working together. Jose loves to draw funny animals and Ariane loves to paint them. First, Jose draws the eyes. They show if the animal is happy, sad, mad, grumpy, or scared. Then he adds the ears, the nose, and the rest of the animal. When his drawings are finished, Ariane paints them bright colors. Ariane and Jose hope the bears in Splash! make you smile.

Look for these other Green Light Readers in affordably priced paperbacks and hardcovers!

Level 1/Kindergarten–Grade 1

Big Brown Bear
David McPhail

Big Pig and Little Pig
David McPhail

Cloudy Day/Sunny Day
Donald Crews

Come Here, Tiger
Alex Moran
Illustrated by Lisa Campbell Ernst

Down on the Farm
Rita Lascaro

Just Clowning Around
Steven MacDonald
Illustrated by David McPhail

Lost!
Patti Trimble
Illustrated by Daniel Moreton

Popcorn
Alex Moran
Illustrated by Betsy Everitt

Rabbit and Turtle Go to School
Lucy Floyd
Illustrated by Christopher Denise

Rip's Secret Spot
Kristi T. Butler
Illustrated by Joe Cepeda

Six Silly Foxes
Alex Moran
Illustrated by Keith Baker

Sometimes
Keith Baker

The Tapping Tale
Judy Giglio
Illustrated by Joe Cepeda

What Day Is It?
Patti Trimble
Illustrated by Daniel Moreton

What I See
Holly Keller

Level 2/Grades 1–2

Animals on the Go
Jessica Brett
Illustrated by Richard Cowdrey

A Bed Full of Cats
Holly Keller

Catch Me If You Can!
Bernard Most

The Chick That Wouldn't Hatch
Claire Daniel
Illustrated by Lisa Campbell Ernst

Digger Pig and the Turnip
Caron Lee Cohen
Illustrated by Christopher Denise

The Fox and the Stork
Gerald McDermott

Get That Pest!
Erin Douglas
Illustrated by Wong Herbert Yee

I Wonder
Tana Hoban

Marco's Run
Wesley Cartier
Illustrated by Reynold Ruffins

The Purple Snerd
Rozanne Lanczak Williams
Illustrated by Mary GrandPré

Shoe Town
Janet Stevens and Susan Stevens Crummel
Illustrated by Janet Stevens

Tumbleweed Stew
Susan Stevens Crummel
Illustrated by Janet Stevens

The Very Boastful Kangaroo
Bernard Most

Why the Frog Has Big Eyes
Betsy Franco
Illustrated by Joung Un Kim

Green Light Readers
For the new reader who's ready to GO!